TO: B

FROM: Grandma
&
Grandpa ... Hi!
Goter

R is for Rocket

Aa Bb Cc Dd Ee Ff
Gg Hh Ii Jj Kk
Ll Mm Nn Oo Pp
Qq Rr Ss Tt Uu
Vv Ww Xx Yy Zz

an ABC book by Tad Hills

schwartz & wade books · new york

Rocket and his friends have fun
learning the alphabet.

Rocket finds **a**corns.

Owl draws **a**n
angry **a**lligator.

Bella **b**alances on a **b**all while
a **b**ig **b**lue butterfly watches.

Owl offers a **c**ookie
and a **c**rayon to a **c**row.

"Now will you stop
cawing?" she asks.

Emma **d**igs a **d**eep hole in the **d**irt near the **d**aisies.

In the **e**vening, **E**mma finds an **e**gg.

Fred frolics with fireflies in the field.

Nobody sees Goose in the tall green grass.

Rocket finds a **h**at on a
hill and puts it on **h**is **h**ead.

It makes **h**im **h**appy.

Bella plays
in the **i**vy.

It's not a good **i**dea.
It makes her **i**tch.

Owl jumps for joy.

She loves
to fly **k**ites.

A ladybug lands on a leaf and listens
to Rocket read a letter from Larry.

A **m**ouse on
a **m**ushroom
shares his
milk.

The waves are **n**oisy.
They make Owl **n**ervous.

Owl is afraid of the **o**cean.

Rocket **p**aints a **p**icture
of a **p**eacock. Owl **p**refers
her **p**umpkin.

It is **q**uiet, and Owl is
cozy under her **q**uilt.
She falls asleep **q**uickly.

Rocket **r**ests by the **r**iver in the **r**ain.

Bella **s**its on a **s**tump.

"I'm glad I have this **s**ock," **s**he **s**ays.

Rocket's teacher sees two tiny turtles.
"Are you twins?" she asks.

Unfortunately, Mr. Barker can't fit **u**nder the **u**mbrella.

Bella climbs a vine to get a better view.

Rocket wonders,
"Is it windy up there?"

Bella plays the **x**ylophone.

"**Y**ou are a wonder," the Little **Y**ellow Bird **y**ells from across the **y**ard. "**Y**ou play with **z**est and **z**eal."

Ah, the wondrous, mighty, gorgeous alphabet.

For **A**nne, **B**ill, and **C**athy

Copyright © 2015 by Tad Hills

All rights reserved. Published in the United States by
Schwartz & Wade Books,
an imprint of Random House Children's Books,
a division of Penguin Random House LLC, New York.
Schwartz & Wade Books and the colophon
are trademarks of Penguin Random House LLC.
Visit us on the Web! randomhousekids.com
Educators and librarians, for a variety of teaching tools,
visit us at RHTeachersLibrarians.com

Library of Congress Cataloging-in-Publication Data
Hills, Tad.
R is for rocket : an ABC book / Tad Hills.
—First edition. pages cm
Summary: Rocket the dog, Bella the squirrel, Owl, and
other friends discover the alphabet, from acorns and an
angry alligator to a zig zag drawn by the Little Yellow Bird.

ISBN 978-0-553-52228-0 (hc)
 ISBN 978-0-553-52229-7 (glb)
ISBN 978-0-553-52230-3 (ebook)
[1. Dogs—Fiction. 2. Animals—Fiction. 3. Alphabet.]
I. Title.
PZ7.H563737 Raaf 2015
[E]—dc23
2014045439
The text of this book is set in Filosofia.
The illustrations were rendered in oil paint,
acrylic, and colored pencil.
MANUFACTURED IN CHINA
10 9 8 7 6 5 4 3 2
First Edition
Random House Children's Books
supports the First Amendment and
celebrates the right to read.